KU-749-357

THE STORY OF IRON MAN

Adapted by **Thomas Macri**
Illustrated by **Craig Rousseau** *and* **Hi-Fi Design**
Based on the Marvel comic book series **Iron Man**

MARVEL
New York

marvelkids.com

TM & © 2013 Marvel & Subs.

Printed in the United States of America

First Edition

1 3 5 7 9 10 8 6 4 2

G658-7729-4-13032

ISBN 978-1-4231-5413-6

SUSTAINABLE
FORESTRY
INITIATIVE

Certified Chain of Custody
Promoting Sustainable Forestry

www.sfiprogram.org
SFI-01415

The SFI label applies to the text stock

Tony Stark was good at making
things. He met with the Army. They
wanted him to help them.

Tony worked in an Army lab. Something exploded! An enemy had attacked.

They wanted Tony to make weapons.
They took him away.

They took him to a cell. He met another prisoner. His name was Yinsen.

Yinsen made things, too.

He put a hand on Tony's shoulder.

Tony's heart was hurt.

Yinsen built something to help. It would keep Tony's heart beating. He would always have to wear it. It would keep him alive.

They also made a suit of armor.
Tony would wear it. It would help
them escape.

Now Tony could break anything.
He smashed through a brick wall.

He fought the whole enemy army.

He won easily.

The enemy was scared.
They ran away.

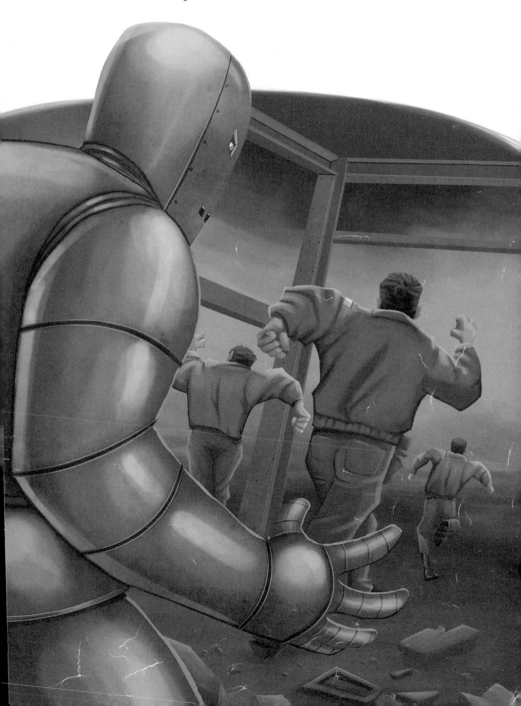

Tony escaped. He used his suit
to fly home.

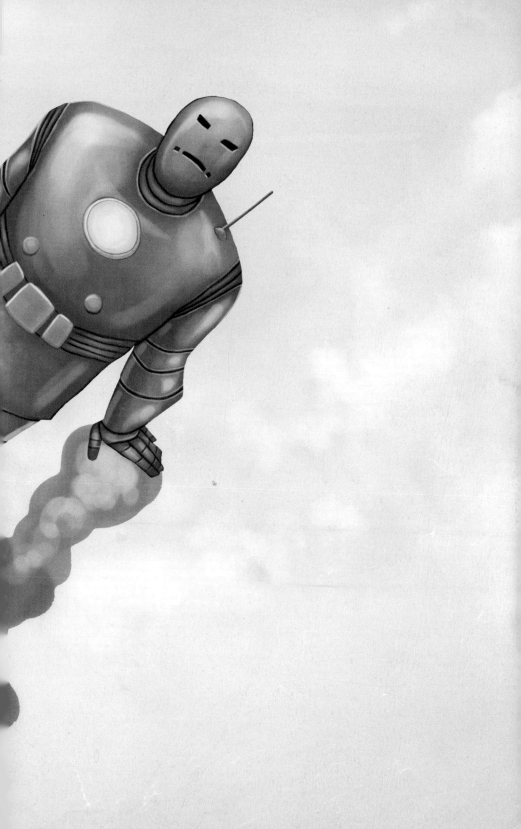

Tony wanted to help others. On TV
he saw a crime happening.

He flew over to help.

Everyone was scared.
The people he was there to save
were scared, too.
His armor was too scary.

Tony painted his armor. Now people would not be scared of him.

His armor was still not perfect.
He still needed to fix it up.

Tony made his suit light.
He painted it red and gold.

He made a powerful energy force.
He shot it from his hands.

He shot it from his boots. The suit could now fly fast.

He had to think of a Super Hero name.
He chose Iron Man.

Iron Man fought Super Villains.

Sometimes he fought two!

He could attack from behind.

He could pick up bad guys.

Tony kept on fixing up the armor. He used special tools. He put on goggles. He worked all the time.

Tony did not always wear a suit
of armor.
Sometimes he wore a suit and tie.

He always kept a suitcase near.
It had his armor inside.

He never knew when the world would need Iron Man!